Pickles

Tru Faith

Illustrated by Daniel Majan

To order additional copies of this book, contact:
Xlibris
1-888-795-4274
www.Xlibris.com
Orders@Xlibris.com

ISBN: Softcover   978-1-7960-5646-4
          EBook   978-1-7960-5645-7

Library of Congress Control Number: 2019913014

Print information available on the last page

Rev. date: 08/30/2019

A family of cucumbers were on their way to the store to pick up some groceries. There was father cucumber named Francis, Mother cucumber named Christy, and their three children, Oliver, Beau, and Violet.

On their way to the grocery store they met up with Bill. Bill was not any ordinary cucumber. He had turned into a pickle. He smelled different, he looked different, and he had a smile on his face all the time. All the other cucumbers wondered what happened to Bill. He seemed to have everything going for him. He did not have a care in the world. He seemed to have life figured out. People envied him. It was as if he never had a problem. But he was friendly and always helped people. He did not act stuck up either like some of the other cucumbers had who lived in the upper country.

Bill happily and politely greeted the cucumber family. Asked them if they needed help with anything. He asked them also if they wanted to be dipped into the vat. The vat was a substance of vinegar and salt that would change them to a pickle.

The father asked Bill why they should be dipped into the vat.

Bill answered the family by stating that by being dipped into the vat they could have everlasting life and have it more abundantly. That they would be a part of a bigger world that even though they had problems had someone to give their problems to.

The cucumber family said that they would have to think about it. Bill invited them to the vat service that was going to be held on the coming up Saturday. The service would explain everything.

The cucumber family left Bill and went on with their shopping. Little Violet asked "What was Bill talking about? And why did he smell so different?"

Christy answered, "There are pickles in this world. They smell different and look slightly different than us because they have been dipped in the vat of vinegar and salt. Bill is one of those cucumbers."

Francis continued Christy's remarks saying that they are different now but they were once like us. They changed. They took on the vat.

Then Violet asked if they were going to the vat. "No," Francis answered, "You have to be a certain age to go into the vat and you have to work for it. At least that is what I was told."

"That does not seem right," Violet answered. "Why can't anyone be a part of the vat? Why does it have to be certain cucumbers?"

"I don't know why, Violet, that is just what I have been told." Her father answered.

"Can we go to the service?" asked Violet.

"I don't think so," answered her father. "We don't belong. We are not the same as them."

As Violet continued asking her father questions they had reached the grocery store and they were getting their groceries when Oliver met his friend, Gertrude, Gert for short.

"Hi Gert," Oliver said to his friend. "How are you doing?"

Gert turned to her friend Oliver and said, "Hello Oliver. How are you doing today? I met this very interesting person over by the vat. I went to the service he talked about and they talked about this other person who could save us. I am so excited. I am going into the vat next week. I cannot wait."

Oliver, in stunned surprise asked, "Why would you do that? Don't you have to be a certain age to go into the vat?"

"Oh no, that is a myth." Gert answered. "Anyone who accepts the Lord can get into the vat."

Oliver had never seen his friend so excited in a long time. She seemed so excited that he could not believe it.

Oliver did not know what his friend was talking about when she said that she had to accept the Lord. She explained that they teach you in the service about the Lord and how he had been stripped of all his earthliness and how he had been hung on a tree for our transgressions. How he had lived a perfect life and that for us to become one with him we would need to accept him totally. Give him our problems and he would forgive us of things we do wrong.

She went on to tell him that they would have to accept him and then they would be able to go into the vat. The vat is just a symbol of acceptance to the Lord.

Oliver was surprised that his dad and mom had never mentioned anything about this before.

Gert went on to tell Oliver about the things she learned in the service. She said "There were many pickles in the world, but they were all different. Some were sweet, some were sour, some were blessed, and some were just plain pickles. You never knew which you would meet. Some of the sour pickles had accepted the Lord but were not very happy with their lives.

"You could tell them by the ones that were the sweet ones because their smell was a little bit different than the sour ones. "The sour pickles tried to tell their story, but it was hard to believe them. They seemed to be just like the other cucumbers in the world. They fit in with the rest of the cucumbers except that they had a slightly different smell. No one could tell the difference between the cucumbers and the sour pickles. They just fit in with the world.

"The regular pickles, well they went to service but did not do anything. They were the ones that would not help anyone. They stated that all they had was enough. They never helped anyone. They did not think they needed to help anyone. They thought they were better somehow than the rest of the pickles.

"Then there are the sweet pickles. These are the happy people. They seem to have no problems in the world. They are always helping people and always are giving things away. Sometimes they seem to give too much, but the Lord has given more than them. He has given his life for them.

Then there are the other pickles, they do some things for others. These pickles go from one kind of pickle to another. They just don't know what way to go. They are sometimes sweet, sometimes regular, and if something bad happens they can turn into a sour pickle.

"The blessed pickles are the ones that will be the ones that help cucumbers into the vat. They are totally into the Lord. These pickles will give their all to further their services to get all cucumbers into the vat. Not every cucumber will want to go into the vat though. This is sad, because once they go into the vat they will last longer.

"Cucumbers will grow weak and will shrivel up and sooner or later will never be seen again. Look at your mother and father, Oliver. They are not getting younger. They are getting older. Soon it will be too late for them to go into the vat. They need to decide soon. For us, we have a while, but I would like to become a better cucumber, so I will be going into the vat this weekend during service time. I cannot wait. It will be better.

"Think about it, Oliver, come with me and go into the vat."

Oliver thought about it. He was thinking about it for a long time. He found his parents and decided to go home to ponder the things Gert had told him.

"Dad, can we go to the service this week? I want to see what it is all about." Oliver asked.

"Oh yea, can we go?" chimed in Little Violet excitedly.

"I don't think so. I don't believe in the same thing they believe. We can work our way and we don't need the vat. There is a lot of ways to go to the Lord. We don't need the vat." Dad answered.

A few weeks later a friend of the cucumber family died. The other cucumbers and pickles in the family came to the funeral. What a nice funeral. Oh, how distraught the cucumber looked. All wrinkled up and looking like he had been through a cucumber slicer. No hope. Nothing. Just a bed of lettuce to lay on. It was over for him. They covered him up with another bed of lettuce and buried him in a traditional cucumber funeral fashion.

Beau asked her mother if the cucumber was going to be with the Lord. Christy replied that she did not know, but the cucumber was a good cucumber so maybe. It is hard to determine if they are going to be with the Lord.

"How can we know if we are going to be with the Lord, mom?" asked Beau. "How can we know if the cucumber went to the Lord?"

"Beau, I really am not sure. But he did good works. He should go to be with the Lord." Mother answered.

Beau now asked if they could go to the vat and to the service on the next Saturday.

Father cucumber replied "No, we are not going to the service on Saturday. We are not going to have any further discussion on this matter. I have spoken."

On Saturday, Oliver snuck out of the house and had gone to the service with Gert. By the time he had gotten to the service, Gert had already entered the vat. She now had a distinctive smell like the other good pickles. It was Oliver's time. He decided to follow his friend Gert. He knew he would be in trouble when he got home, but it did not matter. He wanted to do what his friend was doing.

Oliver had gone with Gert and had disobeyed his father. He also had been dipped in the vat and now was a pickle. He no longer was like his parents and his sisters.

Oliver had felt better. His dad had not accepted his disobedience and was not happy about it. Oliver would have to accept any punishment that his dad would deliver.

New to the Lord, Oliver was not sure how to approach his parents. He received a new book and he was reading it every day. He had no idea that life could be so neat as a pickle.

When Oliver got home, he ran into his little sister, Violet. Violet said to Oliver, "Why do you stink? What did you do?"

Oliver found his parents and insisted that mother, father, and sisters go to be dipped into the vat. He was so excited that he did not even notice that his father, mother, and sisters were backing away from his new smell.

Printed in the United States
By Bookmasters